Dedicated to my son, AJ, who has become a voracious reader:

*For all of your years of patience and respect while being pounced on, slept on, and sometimes scratched by several felines over the years. I'll always remember how you played with GG into the wee hours of the night when she first came to live with us. Thank you for your gentle and tender heart towards my feline friends, even though you **may have had** an allergy to cats.*

The Cat in the Tub
by Barbara J. Collins

Written and designed in the United States of America.

ISBN: 978-1-62620-573-4

This book was created using the Blurb creative publishing service.

To the parents of wee ones:

Young children love to have someone read to them. I remember many fond moments with my son as he'd sit on my lap while I read to him. As an educator, I have always enjoyed reading great literature with my students. These opportunities offer preschool children many benefits. As you read to your children, with enthusiasm, they internalize your enjoyment and claim it for themselves. As they hear story after story read, and reread many times, children develop a true love for reading. Soon they will learn to read themselves. I also believe there is something special about holding a real book and turning the pages together with a child. Call me old fashioned, but I prefer a real book to an electronic book.

The Cat in the Tub

For the past five years, I've taught a literature unit in my preschool. I always included a week of Caldecott winners and another week of Dr. Seuss books. Personally, like many others, I have always loved Dr. Seuss books. While enjoying GG's "kitten-hood", and my love of photography, this book almost begged to be written and shared with my students. Children love the rhyming words in books and I wanted them to learn, even at that young age, that anyone can become an author. While reading this book to my students, it was their giggles and smiles that encouraged me to publish it. I pray many children, and families, will enjoy it for years to come.

The Cat in the Tub

by Ms. Barb, Bub

Most cats don't like to get wet
But you haven't seen GG yet.

This cat doesn't wear a hat
She loves water. Imagine that!

Ever since she was a wee little kit
She loved the water more than a little bit.

The good thing is we don't have any fish
But one day, she wanted to get washed with a dish.

(That's right she is in the dishwasher! Swish swish!)

She even used to sleep in a drippy sink
And when wet, she wouldn't even blink.

No! No! Not the water under the Christmas tree
Will she drink it? I guess we'll see!

(No, she couldn't leave it be.)

Sometimes she watches out the window
Is she looking for rain, or even snow?

Water can be wet, or frozen? Ho! Ho!
Does she really know? She must know!

In the water she puts both feet.
Don't you think she should have a seat?

She even has toys that are rubber ducks
The good thing is they aren't woodchucks!

She tries to get them with her paws
Sometimes she stabs them with her claws.

But, if a toy is on the side
She knocks it off with pride!

She likes to smack it….Whack-o!
I say, "Hey, please put it back-o!"

One day, she reached for a duck.
Then she ran out of luck
She got herself stuck.

She just didn't know what to think,
So, you guessed it, she fell in the drink!

I thought the water made her too slick
But she said, "No problem. I can lick!"

I love her dearly and she is such a cute pet
She is the definitely the silliest I've ever met!

About GG:

In June of 2009, the director of my school shared a photo with me that she had taken of this adorable kitten. She was hoping someone would adopt her that day because her siblings had already found their "forever homes". She pleaded, "I'd hate to see her spend, yet, another weekend by herself in that crate." Her siblings, and she, had been taken from their mom at about 3 weeks of age. She was living in a veterinarian's office where they had been hand feeding them through bottles. When I heard the story my heart melted, since I too had fed kittens, as a teenager. (Our cat had delivered 6 kittens on a Wednesday afternoon, and was deathly ill by Saturday morning. She had a terrible infection and needed to stay in the veterinarian's office for several days. By the time she returned to her kittens, her milk was dried up. I guess the vet knew that would happen because that Saturday, I learned how to feed kittens.)

What GG didn't know was that she had a big brother at home. My nine year old Sweetie Petey was an orange tabby. In a very short time he accepted her although she'd gobble up his food as often as she could. Within two years, I heard that awful word by the veterinarian. GG had become obese. I want to assure you that, much like her human mother, she was put on a weight loss plan. Thankfully we have indeed both lost a healthy amount of weight. She is now three years old and continues to entertain us with her very unusual feline self.

Barbara J. Collins has been an educator for 30 years. Barb has always loved sharing great literature with young children. At one time she owned and operated a licensed daycare from her home. While working at The Goddard School she wrote this book to celebrate Dr. Seuss' birthday. Her goal was to continue his style of writing and show the children anyone can become an author.

She lives in Columbia, MD with her family.

Barb enjoys many other creative pursuits, including creating a sequel to this book.